To Sergey

First published 2013 by Macmillan Children's Books, a division of Macmillan Publishers Limited. 20 New Wharf Road, London N1 9RR. Basingstoke and Oxford. Associated companies throughout the world. www.panmacmillan.com. ISBN: 978-0-230-75464-5 (HB). ISBN: 978-0-230-75465-2 (PB). Text and illustrations copyright © Ekaterina Trukhan 2013. Moral rights asserted.
A CIP catalogue record for this book is available from the British Library. Printed in China.

Ekaterina Trukhan

PATRICK WANTS A DOG!

MACMILLAN CHILDREN'S BOOKS

Patrick wanted a dog.

He dreamed of long walks
in the park and big
doggy cuddles.

But when he asked his parents, sometimes they didn't hear him,

sometimes they were too busy,

and sometimes they said "maybe".

But they never said "yes".

So Patrick decided that if they
wouldn't get him a dog . . .

he'd go out and find one himself.

He gathered together all the things he'd need,

and packed them in his dog-finding kit.

He put on his favourite sweater . . .

and then he was off on his adventure!

WOOF

WOOF

First Patrick looked
in the park.

GRRRR

But all the dogs
there had owners.

So he went to the playground.
Patrick searched high,

and low.

But he didn't
find any dogs.

Next he tried
the pet shop.

There were
lots of
animals . . .

but not one single dog!

Then suddenly Patrick saw a tail!

But he wasn't interested in cats.
And they weren't interested in him.

Patrick was fed up.
Patrick was hungry.
Patrick wanted to go home.

He walked up
and down,
and round
and round . . .

but he was lost!

First Patrick couldn't find a dog,
now he couldn't find his way home.

And just when he thought that things couldn't get any worse . . .

a shadow crept slowly up the wall.
It was . . .

A MONSTER!

Patrick ran as fast as he could.
But the monster followed him!

It was so fast! They ran
until Patrick couldn't run any more.

He could feel the monster's
warm breath getting closer.

It opened its mouth wide . . .

. . . and gave Patrick a big, sloppy lick.

Patrick was so relieved! He wasn't going to
be eaten, and he'd found his way home.

But best of all . . .

. . . he got what he'd always wanted.

And Monster
got a home too.